Katie Woo

Best Season Ever

by Fran Manushkin

illustrated by Tammie Lyon

PICTURE WINDOW BOOKS

a capstone imprint

Katie Woo is published by Picture Window Books,
A Capstone Imprint
151 Good Counsel Drive, P.O. Box 669
Mankato, Minnesota, MN 56002
www.capstonepub.com

Printed in the United States of America in Stevens Point, Wisconsin.
062010
005851R

Library of Congress Cataloging-in-Publication Data
Manushkin, Fran.
   Best season ever / by Fran Manushkin; illustrated by Tammie Lyon.
   p. cm. — (Katie Woo)
   ISBN 978-1-4048-5730-8 (library binding)
   [1. Seasons—Fiction. 2. Friendship—Fiction. 3. Chinese Americans—Fiction.]
I. Lyon, Tammie, ill. II. Title.
PZ7.M3195Bes 2010   2009030611
[E]—dc22

Summary: Katie and her friends Pedro and JoJo disagree over which season of the year is the best.

Art Director: Kay Fraser
Graphic Designer: Emily Harris
Production Specialist: Michelle Biedscheid

Photo Credits
Fran Manushkin, pg. 26
Tammie Lyon, pg. 26

Table of Contents

Chapter 1

Springtime!

It was springtime!

Bluebirds were singing.

And tulips were blooming

their heads off.

"This is my favorite

season," yelled Katie. "No

more winter coats!"

"I like winter!" said Pedro.
"I miss sledding and tossing
snowballs."

"I'd rather throw

beach balls," JoJo

said. "Summer's

a lot more fun."

"No!" said Katie firmly.
"Spring is best! It's not too
hot and not too cold. It's
perfect for jumping rope and
roller skating."

"But summer is more tasty!" JoJo insisted. "I love roasting hot dogs and eating ice cream."

"You can eat ice cream and hot dogs anytime," said Katie. "But you can only see apple blossoms in spring."

Chapter 2

Favorite Seasons

Katie climbed the apple

tree to smell the blossoms.

When she climbed down, Katie said, "Autumn is my second favorite season. I love Halloween!"

"Trick-or-treating is great," agreed Pedro. "And running around, kicking a soccer ball."

"Running barefoot in the sand at the beach is better," said JoJo. "Summer is more fun at night too. You can see fireflies."

"And bugs that bite!"

yelled Pedro.

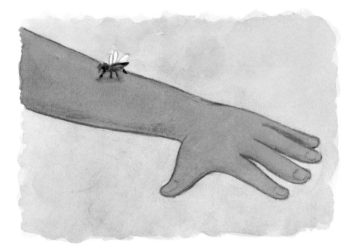

"And shooting stars!"

said Katie.

"And stinging jellyfish!"

groaned Pedro.

"Race you!" yelled Katie.

The three friends ran like the wind! When they reached a puddle, Katie gave it a kick.

"Pedro, isn't this fun? Spring is much better than winter!" yelled Katie. "Why are you so stubborn?"

"Who's stubborn?" yelled
Pedro. He gave the puddle
such a big kick that water
splashed on Katie's face.

"You did that
on purpose!" Katie
yelled.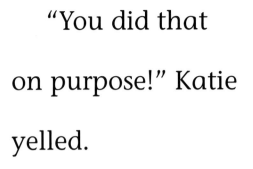

"No I didn't!"

Pedro insisted.

As he began running

away, he dropped his book.

He bent down to pick it up.

"Ribbit!" shouted JoJo,
jumping over him. "Let's
play leapfrog."

"Ribbit!" Pedro croaked,
leaping over JoJo.

Chapter 3

Katie Makes Up Her Mind

Katie began jumping
rope. It was fun showing off,
jumping faster and faster!

Whoops! Katie tripped
and fell down — right on top
of Pedro and JoJo.

Their arms and legs got
all tangled up.

"Look at us!" JoJo giggled.
"We are an octopus!"

"Katie, did you do that on
purpose?" asked Pedro.

"No!" Katie insisted. "But

this is on purpose."

She picked four wild

daffodils . . .

. . . and gave them to Pedro

and JoJo.

"Thanks!" they said.

"Guess what?" Katie told
them. "I've made up my
mind. All of the seasons are
fun when I'm with you."

"For sure!" Pedro and JoJo agreed.

"Let's go to my house for hot chocolate," Katie said.

"Cold chocolate ice cream tastes better," teased Pedro.

And they joked about it

all the way home.

About the Author

Fran Manushkin is the author of many popular picture books, including *How Mama Brought the Spring; Baby, Come Out!; Latkes and Applesauce: A Hanukkah Story;* and *The Tushy Book*. There is a real Katie Woo — she's Fran's great-niece — but she never gets in half the trouble of the Katie Woo in the books. Fran writes on her beloved Mac computer in New York City, without the help of her two naughty cats, Cookie and Goldy.

About the Illustrator

Tammie Lyon began her love for drawing at a young age while sitting at the kitchen table with her dad. She continued her love of art and eventually attended the Columbus College of Art and Design, where she earned a bachelors degree in fine art. After a brief career as a professional ballet dancer, she decided to devote herself full time to illustration. Today she lives with her husband, Lee, in Cincinnati, Ohio. Her dogs, Gus and Dudley, keep her company as she works in her studio.

Glossary

autumn (AW-tuhm)—the season between summer and winter, from September to December

barefoot (BAIR-fut)—without shoes or socks

blossoms (BLOSS-uhms)—flowers on a fruit tree or other plant

chocolate (CHOK-uh-lit)—a type of candy made from ground roasted cacao beans

daffodils (DAF-uh-dils)—yellow bell-like flowers

favorite (FAY-vuh-rit)—the thing you like best

groaned (GROHND)—made a long low sound to show unhappiness

insisted (in-SIS-tid)—demanded very firmly

stubborn (STUHB-urn)—not willing to give in or change; set on having your own way

Discussion Questions

1. What is your favorite season?

2. What is your least favorite season?

3. Katie, Pedro, and JoJo disagreed about which season was the best one. Have you ever disagreed with a friend? What happened?

Writing Prompts

1. Choose one of the four seasons and research it. Write a paragraph that includes the following information: the months, type of weather, and holidays of the season.

2. In the book, the three friends talk about their favorite activities for each season. Draw a picture of you doing your favorite activity during your favorite season. Write a sentence about your picture.

3. List five things that describe your favorite season.

Having Fun
with Katie Woo

In *Best Season Ever*, Katie Woo argues with her friends about which season is the best. Which season do you think is best? Create a poster to let everyone know why your season is so great!

What you need:

- scratch paper and pen
- large white tag board
- crayons, markers, or paints

What you do:

1. Think of your favorite season. What makes it the best season ever? List the things that make your season special on scratch paper. If your season was summer, you might list ice cream, the beach, and swimming.

2. Using a marker, crayon, or paint, write a headline about your season across the top of the tag board. "Winter is #1" is an example. Use bright colors and big letters to make your headline stand out.

3. Draw a seasonal scene. Include details from your list from step one. For example, a summer poster could show a girl building a castle at the beach and a boy eating ice cream. Take your time and make it neat.

Be sure to hang up your finished poster so everyone can see your best season ever!